I'm a little
MONSTER

For Kelly and Matthew

This paperback edition first published in 2001 by Andersen Press Ltd. The rights of Sandy Nightingale to be identified as the author and illustrator of this work have been asserted by her in accordance with the Copyright, Designs and Patents Act, 1988. First published in Great Britain in 1994 by Andersen Press Ltd., 20 Vauxhall Bridge Road, London SW1V 2SA. Published in Australia by Random House Australia Pty., 20 Alfred Street, Milsons Point, Sydney, NSW 2061.

Printed and bound in China.

10 9 8 7 6 5 4 3 2 1

British Library Cataloguing in Publication Data available.

ISBN 0 86264 502 6

This book has been printed on acid-free paper

I'm a little
MONSTER

Words and pictures by Sandy Nightingale

Ⓐ
Andersen Press • London

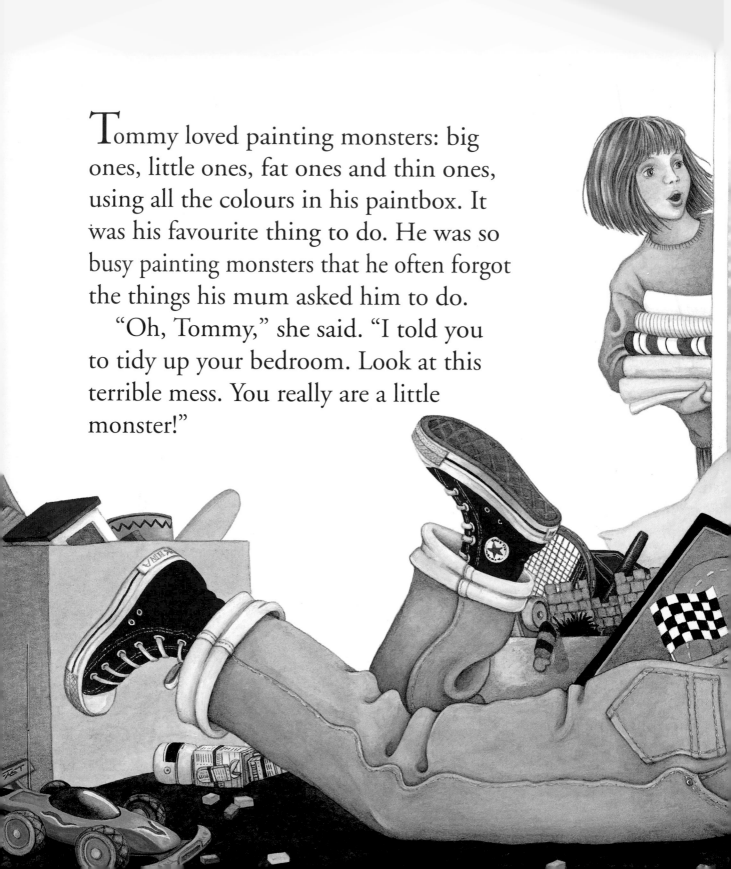

Tommy loved painting monsters: big ones, little ones, fat ones and thin ones, using all the colours in his paintbox. It was his favourite thing to do. He was so busy painting monsters that he often forgot the things his mum asked him to do.

"Oh, Tommy," she said. "I told you to tidy up your bedroom. Look at this terrible mess. You really are a little monster!"

Tommy began to tidy his
toys away. He didn't like
his mum to be cross.

"I'm not a little monster,"
he said to himself.

"No, but we are," called
a strange voice.

Tommy stared at the picture he had
just painted.
    He couldn't believe his eyes.

The monsters were smiling
and waving

and getting BIGGER
and BIGGER.

Until they climbed right
out of the book.

"Hello, Tommy," said the little green monster.
"Where am I?" gasped Tommy, gazing around.
"This is the land you painted for us," replied the monster.

Tommy stared in wonder.

"My name's Grobbler," the little monster went on, "and here are my friends Snoot, Gobbalina, Smeepoo, Birdbrain, Blurp and Pog the Dog. Come and meet my mum."

"I'm very pleased to meet you, Tommy," welcomed Grobbler's mum. "My little monster has told me all about you."

"My mum calls me a little monster too," said Tommy.

"She sounds very nice," smiled Grobbler's mum approvingly. "Would you like to stay for Grobbler's birthday party?"

"Oh, yes please," said Tommy.

"Hurray!" cried Grobbler. "Come and choose a costume from the dressing-up box. It's going to be a fancy dress party."

Grobbler's mum made a wonderful birthday tea.

There was a lovely wobbly jelly and a beautiful birthday cake.

But first of all they played all sorts of party games.

Tommy thought it was much more fun playing with monsters.

When they sat down to tea, some of the monsters
ate their plates and napkins as well as the food.
   "Saves washing up," said Grobbler's mum cheerfully.

One even ate the candles on the birthday cake.
"Well, after all, they are monsters," thought Tommy.

Grobbler gave Tommy a big hug.

"I'm so glad you came to my party," he said.

"So am I," agreed Tommy. "But I'm sorry I didn't bring you a present."

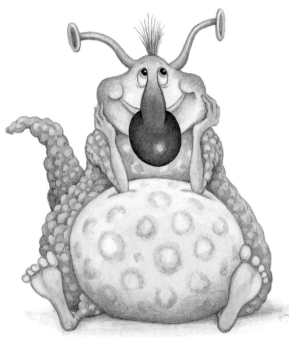

"There is something you could give me," said Grobbler shyly. "Next time you do some painting, could you paint a beautiful red bicycle for me?"

"Of course I will," laughed Tommy. "I promise."

Just then, very faintly, Tommy
heard a familiar voice calling his name.

"Tommy! Tommy!"

"Mum!" called Tommy. "I'm here." And he ran
towards the voice. Suddenly he was in his own room again.

"Tommy, you still haven't tidied your room," said his mum. "Honestly, you really are ..."

"I know," said Tommy with a big grin.

"I'm a little MONSTER!"